Bat-Oren
The Good Deed Balloon

Illustrations: Yonat Katzir

Bat-Oren

The Good Deed Balloon

Illustrations: Yonat Katzir

One morning, about two weeks before the holidays, posters suddenly appeared all over town –

A long line of people and animals gathered even before the balloon had landed. They were all sure they'd done a good deed and they all wanted to fly in the balloon.

It was a clear sunny day, not a cloud in the deep blue sky.
The first to arrive were a rabbit and a frog.
The rabbit lived in a burrow under the lawn and the frog had quickly moved to a nearby pond before the balloon arrived.
When the balloon basket landed on the grass they all ran up.

Suddenly a loud voice echoed: "What's all this? What's the rush? Get in line fast!" Nobody saw who gave the order but they all obeyed.
"The first two, approach the basket!" the voice ordered.
Trembling, the rabbit and the frog came closer.

"Why do you think you deserve to fly in the Good Deed Balloon?" Came the voice. The frog jumped in the air and said: "I pushed a fish back into the water after it came ashore by mistake."

The rabbit raised his ears and said: "And I pulled a thorn out of an elephant's leg in the circus!"
"Please get in," invited the voice, and the two immediately jumped into the basket.

Next in line were a fox and a raven. In his hoarse voice, the raven claimed he'd found a robin's chick that had fallen from its nest and he'd returned it.

The fox said: "I went into a vineyard and though I was hungry I didn't steal any grapes." "That doesn't count!" thundered the voice, "do not get in!"

The fox stood to one side with his tail drooping and the raven flew up into the basket.

A grey lizard raised her head and said:"
I helped the ants carry seeds to their
ant heap."
The porcupine lowered his needles
and said bashfully:"And I carried a
turtle on my back and we crossed the
road together."

"Well done both of you, in you get," said the voice. The lizard and the porcupine climbed slowly up the ladder.

A ginger cat and a black Labrador were next.
The dog said: "I rescued a boy who fell out of
a boat into the river."
The cat told how he'd seen a mouse in the
yard and hadn't chased it.

"That doesn't count," said the voice, "stand aside."
The cat howled and yowled but it didn't help, and the dog climbed in.

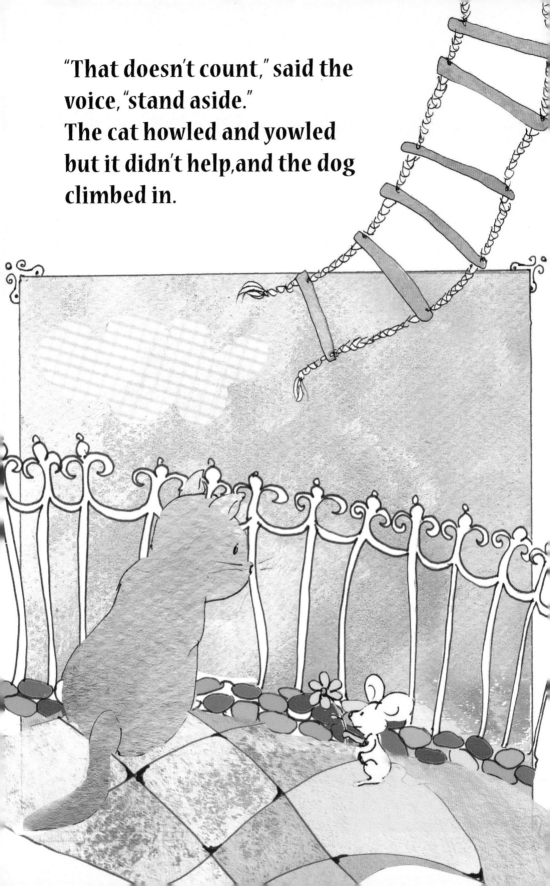

Finally it was the turn of the humans. One girl with freckles and two braids told how she'd walked an old lady home and helped her carry her bag. A taxi driver said: "I took a homeless person to my place and found him a job!" The girl and the driver climbed up the ladder and joined the animals already waiting there.

Last but not least were a postman on his bicycle and a cashier lady from the store. The postman said: "Yesterday I brought a telegram with bad news and stayed to comfort the family."

The cashier lady said that one day a man in the queue was fifty pence short, and she paid it from her own purse. Naturally, both of them were invited in and now the basket was full.

The flame under the balloon grew stronger and the flying balloon filled up with air and slowly rose while the people and animals on the ground clapped their hands and paws. It flew over the tree tops to hover in the blue sky as a flock of robins flew by.

Every passenger was given binoculars and down below they could see an elephant slowly raising a leg in greeting, an old woman and a boy waving, and a turtle lifting its head. As the balloon cruised over the river a fish swished its tail and sunrays shone silver on its scales.

So, my friends, if you know any people or animals who have done good deeds, won't you write their names at the bottom of the page and next time the balloon lands in your neighborhood, they will also be invited to fly in the Good Deed Balloon.

Good Deed

Name: _____

Good Deed:

Translation & Editing: Noel Canin
Illustrations: Yonat Katzir

Printed in Great Britain
by Amazon